Be proud of who you are
and always stay true to yourself.
– Ellen

For all the "foxes" in my life.
– Agnes

Copyright © 2021 Clavis Publishing Inc., New York

Visit us on the Web at www.clavis-publishing.com.

A New Home for Fox written by Ellen DeLange and illustrated by Agnes Ofner

ISBN 978-1-60537-645-5

This book was printed in July 2021 at Drukarnia Perfekt S. A., ul. Połczyńska 99, 01-303 Warszawa, Poland.

First Edition
10 9 8 7 6 5 4 3 2 1

Written by Ellen DeLange
Illustrated by Agnes Ofner

A New Home for Fox

Clavis

NEW YORK

Early in the morning, while still sleeping in his den,
Fox is suddenly disturbed by a pack of dogs.
The dogs are so close, he hears them sniffing.

Fox has no time to think, he gets up and runs.
He barely escapes; fortunately his den has another exit.

Fox keeps looking over his shoulder.
He can still hear the dogs barking.
With his tongue hanging out of his mouth,
he runs, panting heavily, through the forest.
After a while the barking of the dogs fades away.
Did he succeed in escaping them?

He lets out a deep sigh . . .
That was quite a scare! Fox thinks.
There he is, all alone, so far from home . . .
He has no idea where he has run to.

He's in a forest, but it isn't his forest.
Exhausted, he closes his eyes and falls
into a deep, deep sleep.

When Fox wakes up, he feels a lot better.
He's excited to explore his new environment.
Where are the other animals? he thinks.

Suddenly he spots something near the briar patch.
What's hidden under that tree? A den?
He softly knocks on the door.

A badger swiftly opens the door; startled to see a fox.
"Go somewhere else with your devious fox pranks!" he shouts.

Fox spots a farmhouse on the edge of the woods.
The chickens in the henhouse run around wildly as he approaches.
"Watch out! A fox!" shrieks a hen.
"Go hide!" shouts the rooster.

Fox stands still and asks, "Can you please tell me where I am?"
But the hen calls out, "You're too cunning for us, go away!"

Then Fox sees a raccoon.
At home he always loved to play with his friend Raccoon.
He runs after the raccoon to see if he also wants to play.

But the raccoon turns around and shouts,
"Leave me alone, you're only after my food."

Fox isn't happy, he only wants to play . . .

Fox passes a small brook and stops to drink some water.
He looks at his reflection and sees two sad eyes staring at him.

*The animals in this unfamiliar forest don't seem to really like me.
But they don't even know me! he thinks. I know I can be cunning
and mischievous sometimes, but that helped me escape the dogs.
However, I'm also kind and caring . . .*

If only there was a way to show the animals in this forest who I really am.

Without thinking, he picks up a small egg that had fallen out of its nest and carefully places it back.

The sun is setting as Fox trudges
through the forest.
He thinks about his good friends
back home.
A tear falls down his cheek.

*If I can't find my way back,
I'll have to make new friends,*
Fox thinks.

Fox decides to make a place
for the night where he can rest
and figure out what to do next.

He finds a nice spot under
the branches of a fir tree.

He digs a hole, nothing like his den at home,
but it'll protect him against the cold for now
and keep him safe.

Most animals in the forest are about to go to sleep.
Fox curls up in his new hole, his thick tail keeps his feet
and nose very warm.

Suddenly he hears a roaring noise . . . It's coming closer . . . Fox opens one eye. The animals run past him, looking very scared. Then he sees a wild boar following closely behind them!

Fox doesn't think twice. He takes the lead and shouts to the animals, "Go hide underneath the fir trees!"

There's no time for Fox to be scared. With the wild boar on his tail,
he has to quickly think of a trick to lure him away.

Scanning his surroundings, he hears streaming water. That gives him an idea.
As fast as he can, he runs up a small hill right next to the river.
He swiftly looks around and decides to hide behind a large rock.

The wild boar rumbles past Fox without noticing him. The animal has lost
the smell of Fox and runs on furiously, without looking left or right.
Then he falls right over the edge of the hill into the fast-flowing water!

Fox's heart pounds as he looks over the edge. In the distance, he sees the wild boar climbing out of the water on the other side of the river. *Pfff . . . he won't be back,* Fox sighs in relief.

One by one the other animals emerge . . .
They're so happy that the wild boar is gone.

"How clever and courageous you are," they say to Fox.
"And resourceful . . . You've managed to scare away the big wild boar.
Now we don't need to be scared anymore." Fox smiles shyly.

Fox explains to them that he got lost when three dogs
were chasing him and that he can't find his way back home.

"I miss my old home and my friends," says Fox sadly.

Now that the forest animals have gotten to know Fox better,
they feel more at ease with him.
"This is your home now," they say to Fox.
"Shall we play later?" asks the raccoon. "But first we have
some work to do."

And all the animals get together to build a new den for Fox.

And Fox . . . he stands on top of a big rock
and looks at his reflection in the water.
This time he sees a twinkle in his eyes.

Fox is already starting to feel at home.

And then he happily runs after the raccoon
as they play together.